# Seven Froggies Went to School

Sever

# Froggies Went to School

## by Kate Duke

E. P. DUTTON · NEW YORK

The text for this book is adapted from a song
Kate Duke's grandmother learned as a child. The
original version is called "Twenty Froggies
Went to School." The words are by George Cooper.

Copyright © 1985 by Kate Duke

All rights reserved.

Published in the United States by E.P. Dutton, Inc.,
2 Park Avenue, New York, N.Y. 10016
Published simultaneously in Canada by
Fitzhenry & Whiteside Limited, Toronto
Editor: Ann Durell    Designer: Isabel Warren-Lynch
Printed in Hong Kong by South China Printing Co.
First Edition    W    10 9 8 7 6 5 4 3 2 1

Library of Congress Cataloging in Publication Data
Duke, Kate.
    Seven froggies went to school.
    Summary: Seven little frogs go to school and
learn some important lessons from Master Bullfrog.
    1. Children's stories, American.    [1. Frogs—Fiction.
2. Behavior—Fiction.    3. Stories in rhyme]    1. Title.
PZ8.3.D876Se    1985    [E]    84-13712
ISBN 0-525-44160-3

to Grammy
from her namesake
with much love

Seven froggies went to school
down beside a rushy pool,
seven little coats of green,
seven vests all white and clean.

"We must be on time," said they.

"First we study, then we play.
That is how to keep the rule..."

when we froggies go to school!"

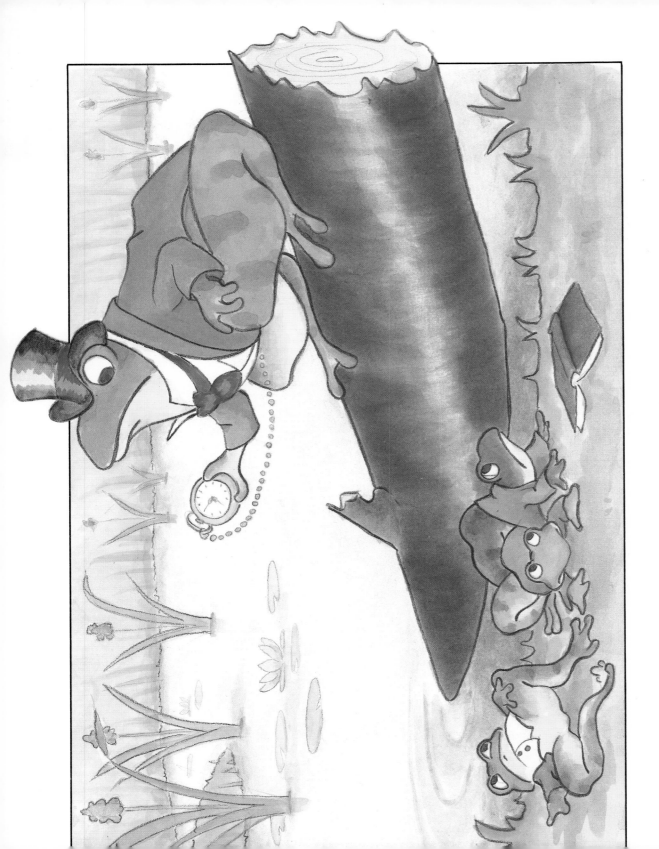

Master Bullfrog, grave and stern,
called the classes in their turn.
From his seat upon a log,
he taught the wisdom of the bog.

"Froggies, hearken to my words!
Stay away from cats and birds,

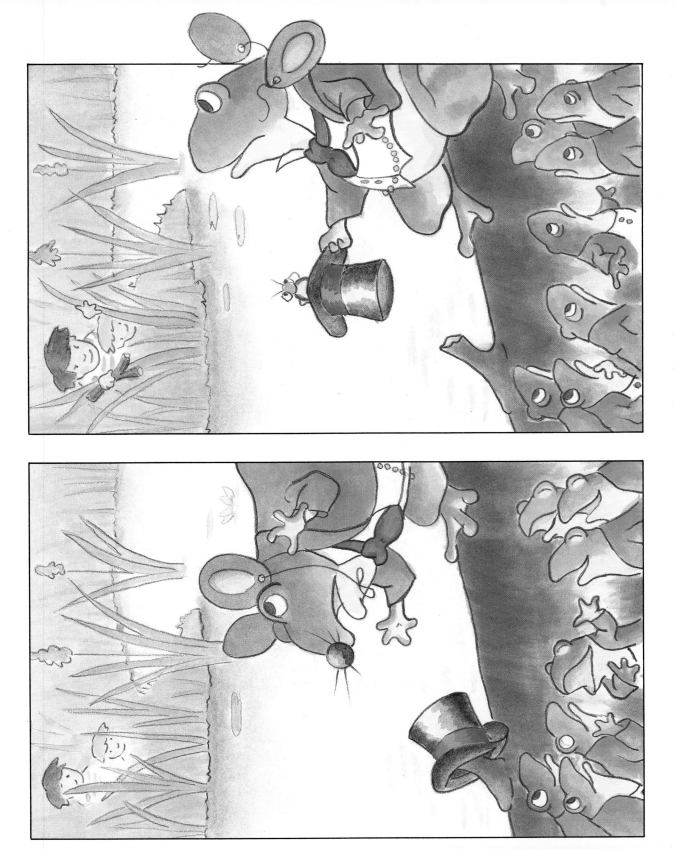

beware the wily muskrat's tricks,
and, froggies, RUN—

from boys with sticks!"

Then all the froggies followed him....

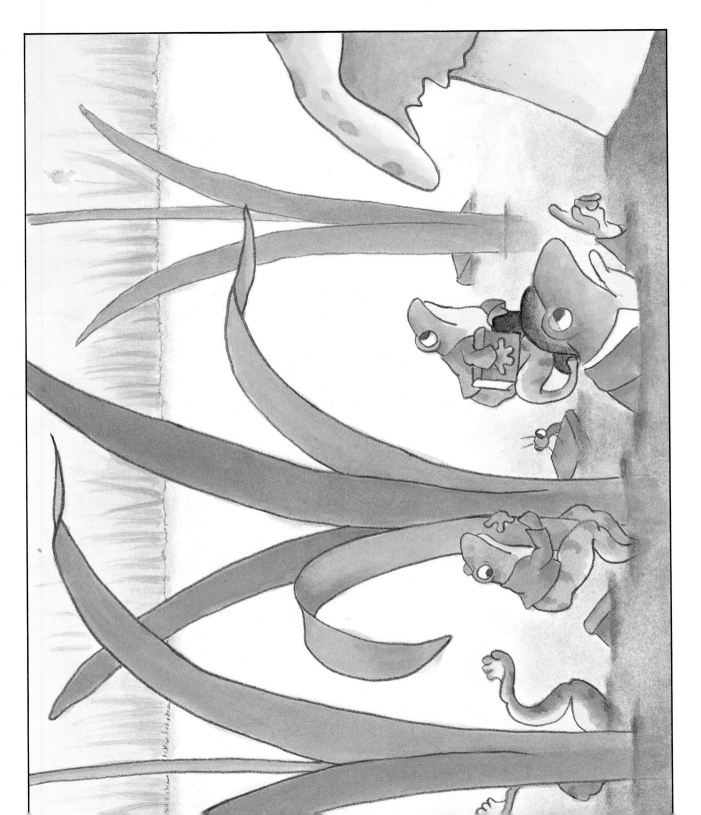

and quickly learned to dive and swim.

They learned to ride upon a newt.

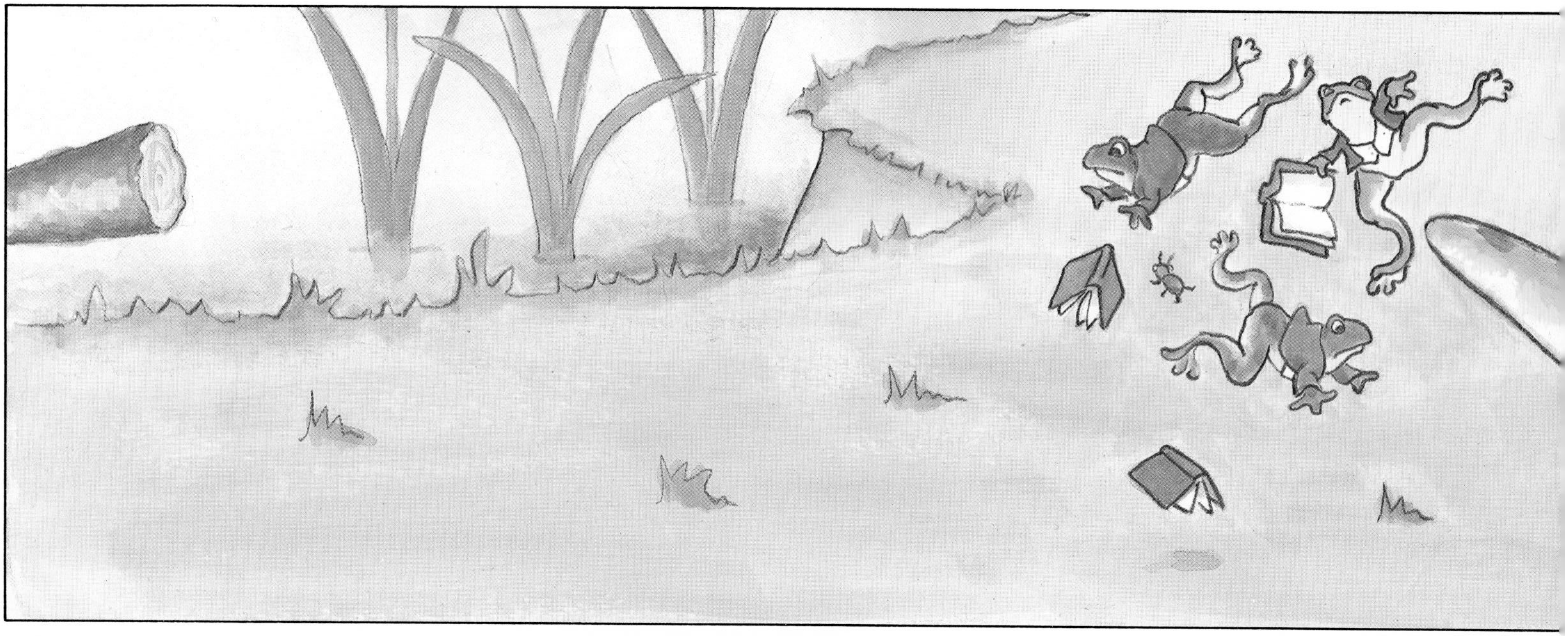

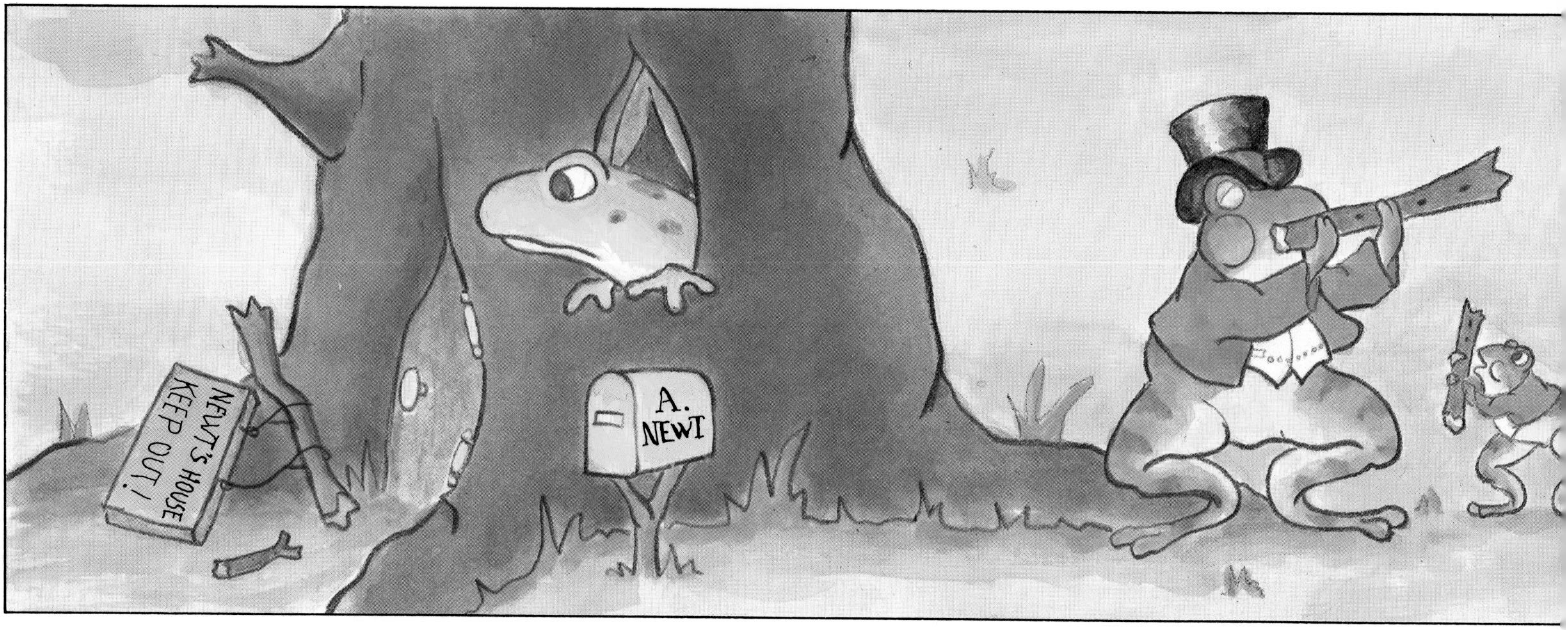
NEWT'S HOUSE
KEEP OUT!
A.
NEWT

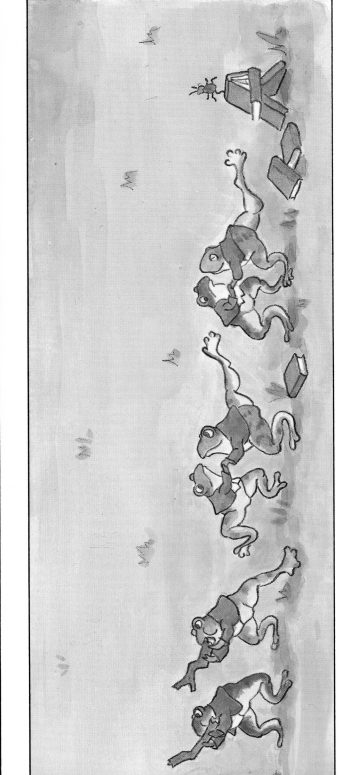

They learned to dance and play the flute.

And when they all had done their best,

Master Bullfrog let them rest.

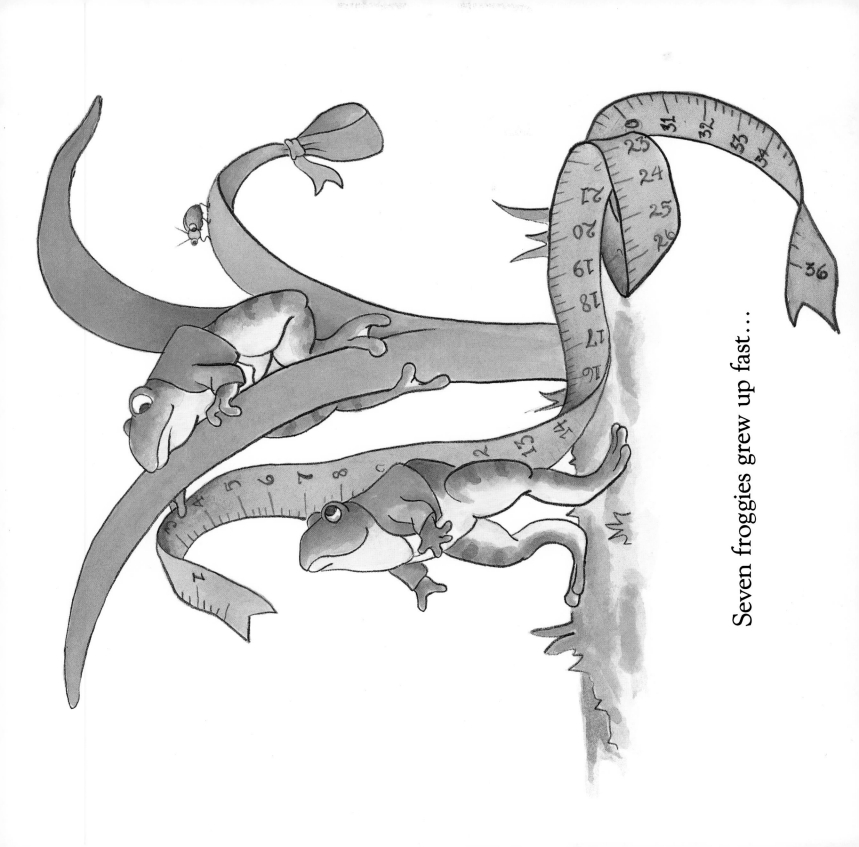

Seven froggies grew up fast...

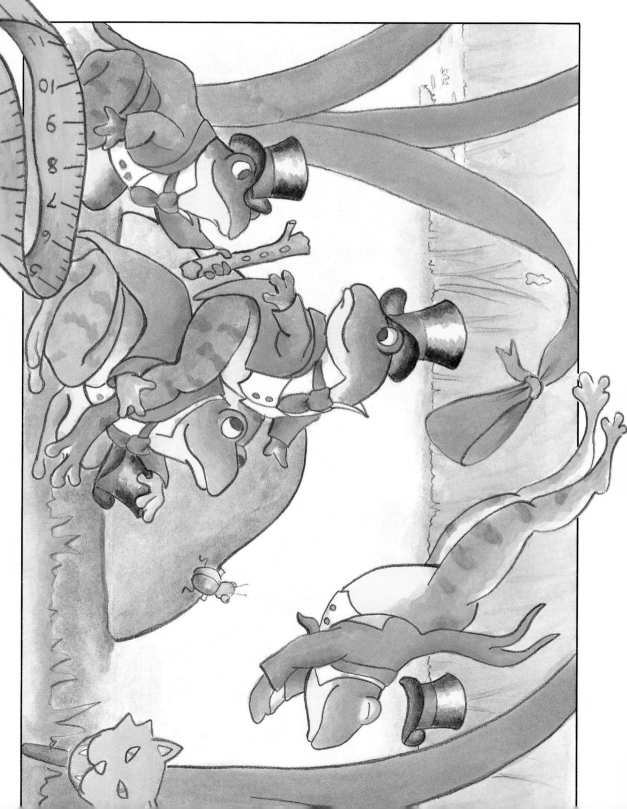

big frogs they became at last,
polished to a high degree
as each froggie ought to be.
Not one dunce among the lot!
Not one lesson they forgot!

They heeded Master Bullfrog's words
regarding pussycats and birds.
By heart they knew the muskrat's tricks,
and how they RAN—

from boys with sticks!

"We've studied long and hard," said they,

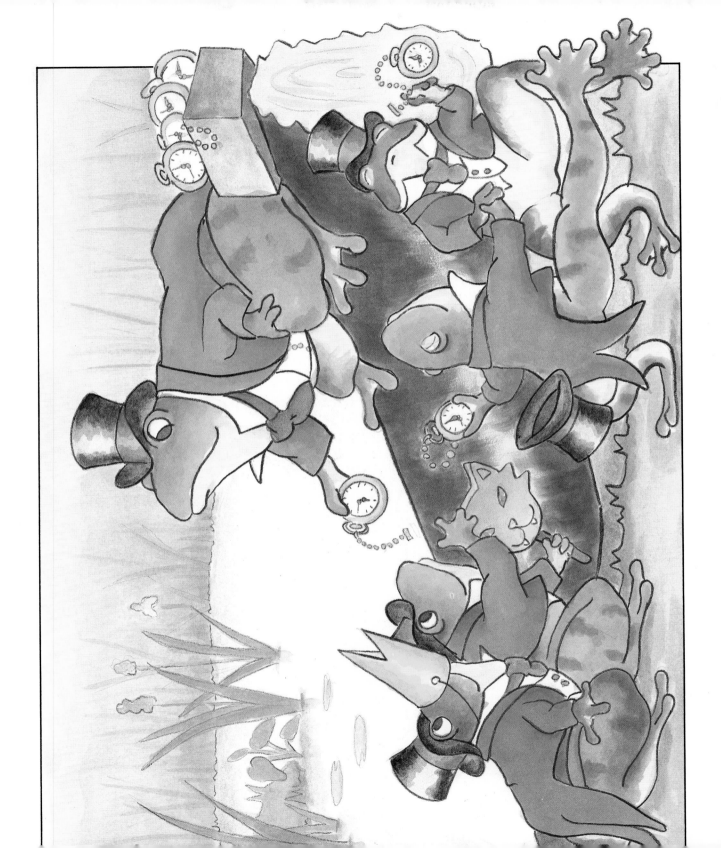

"and come to school on time each day."

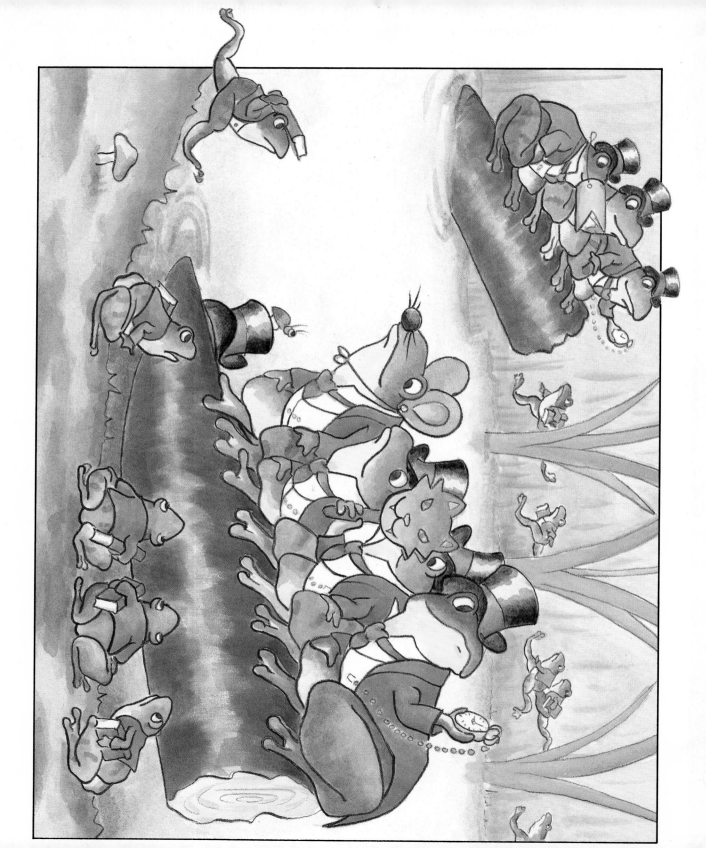

Now they sit on other logs,
teaching other little frogs.